"Give me back my vegetables—you potato nose!" shrieks the wee small woman after hungry Giant Rumbleton comes rumbling into her garden. Insults and legumes fly through the air, until the giant, really a gentle soul, hangs his head in shame and offers to help plant a fresh patch. The pair strikes up an unlikely friendship by sharing a big steaming pot of vegetable soup while the giant sings the happy "Soup for Supper" song, the music for which you'll find on the last page.

Sue Truesdell's exuberant illustrations bring out all the energy and fun of this new folktale.

This is a Junior Literary Guild selection, chosen as an outstanding book for boys and girls (P Group).

*Book Club
Edition*

Soup for Supper

Soup for Supper

by Phyllis Root

illustrated by Sue Truesdell

Harper & Row, Publishers

Soup for Supper
Text copyright © 1986 by Phyllis Root
Illustrations copyright © 1986 by Susan G. Truesdell
Song: Lyrics by Phyllis Root
Music by Linda Sanders
Copyright © 1986 by Phyllis Root and Linda Sanders
Printed in the U.S.A. All rights reserved.
Designed by Trish Parcell
10 9 8 7 6 5 4 3 2 1
First Edition

Library of Congress Cataloging-in-Publication Data
Root, Phyllis.
Soup for supper.

Summary: A wee small woman catches a giant taking
the vegetables from her garden and finds that they can
share both vegetable soup and friendship.
[1. Giants—Fiction.   2. Vegetables—Fiction.
3. Soups—Fiction]   I. Truesdell, Sue, ill.   II. Title.
PZ7.R6784So 1986   [E]   85-45273
ISBN 0-06-025070-4
ISBN 0-06-025071-2 (lib. bdg.)

To my mother and father, with love
P.R.

For Uncle Eric and Aunt Peggy
S.T.

A wee small woman lived all by herself with only her garden for company.

"And how are my cabbages today?" she would say as she checked their leaves for slugs.

"Are my carrots thirsty?" she asked while she tenderly watered the rows.

"Here, little rutabagas, let me shade your roots," she said, tucking mulch up close to their stems.

1

One day the wee small woman was weeding her onion patch when she heard a giant coming over the hill. KA-RUMBLE, KA-RUMBLE, the ground shook with every step. The wee small woman hid behind her mulberry bush to watch the giant pass by.

But Giant Rumbleton stopped and sniffed the air with his enormous nose. "Ho, ho," he chuckled. "My eyes may be weak, but my nose knows a carrot when it smells one." He sniffed again. "Potatoes, too. This is my lucky day."

He put down his cart and set to work.

"These feel like wee small vegetables to me," he rumbled as he pulled them up. "Still, they will make a fine pot of soup for supper." Then he sang in a thunderous voice:

"Soup, soup, soup, a delicious pot of soup,
Soup, soup, soup, I will eat it with a scoop—
Soup for supper tonight."

"Here, stop that!" cried the wee small woman, running out from behind the bush and flapping her wide, wide apron. "Those are *my* vegetables!"

> "*Soup with parsnips, soup with peas,*
> *Soup with rutabagas, please,*"

sang the giant as he dug up her garden.

Then he wheeled his cart on down the road with the wee small woman scurrying behind.

"Give me back my vegetables!" she shouted as loudly as she could.

"Did I hear something?" the giant wondered.

"Give me back my vegetables—you potato nose!" the wee small woman shrieked.

"Potato nose! Who's calling me a potato nose?" Giant Rumbleton bellowed. And he scooped up a handful of potatoes from the cart and flung them around.

The wee small woman gathered up the potatoes in her wide, wide apron and hurried off down the road after the giant.

"Give me back my cabbages! Give me back my beets, you cauliflower head!" she cried.

"What? A cauliflower head? Who are you? Where are you?" yelled the giant. He squinted up into the trees. He blinked at the bushes.

"Nobody calls me names," he shouted, grabbing a dozen cauliflowers and pelting them about.

The wee small woman dodged the cauliflowers, then quickly picked them up and tossed them into her wide, wide apron. She ran after the giant again.

"Those vegetables are *mine*!" she screeched. "Give them back, old rutabaga ears!"

"Rutabaga ears!" roared the giant. "I'll give you rutabaga ears!" He pitched rutabaga after rutabaga wildly from the cart.

The wee small woman gathered up the rutabagas in her wide, wide apron.

"Give them *all* back, carrot toes!" she shouted.

Giant Rumbleton was very proud of his feet
and the noise they made when he walked, and
this made him more angry than anything else.
He grabbed up all the vegetables in the cart
and hurled them through the air.

The wee small woman picked them all up
and put them into her apron. Then she trudged
slowly back up the road toward her cottage.

"No soup for supper," Giant Rumbleton
muttered as he stared at his empty cart. So
off he went, KA-RUMBLE, KA-RUMBLE, back up
the road to find some more vegetables. Soon
the smell of potatoes, cauliflowers, carrots,
and rutabagas drifted past his nose.

"So you've come back, have you?" a wee small voice shouted up at him as he rounded a bend. "Well, you won't get my vegetables *again*."

The giant kneeled down to peer at the wee small woman. "*Your* vegetables?" he puzzled. "I didn't know they belonged to you. I only wanted a fine pot of soup for supper."

"Soup, is it?" she snapped.

The wee small woman looked at the giant's empty cart. Then she looked at her wide, wide apron full of vegetables, which was getting very heavy.

"Carry these home for me," she said, "and I'll cook you up a pot of the finest soup you've ever tasted."

So Giant Rumbleton loaded all the vegetables into his cart, and loaded up the wee small woman as well, and bundled them back up the road to her cottage, singing:

"Soup with onions, soup with parsley,
Soup with pepper sprinkled sparsely."

There the two of them scraped and
scrubbed and peeled and sliced the vegetables.

Thwack, thwack, thwack went the wee
small woman's knife as she diced potatoes.

Tha-wunk, tha-wunk went the giant's knife
as he chopped up a rutabaga.

"Watch out, you turnip brain," the wee
small woman scolded as the giant just missed
chopping her fingers. "Do I look like a bunch
of carrots to you?"

"I'm sorry," the giant rumbled sadly. "I
can't see very well."

"Horseradish!" snorted the wee small woman as she dropped all the chopped vegetables into her wash kettle. "Even a bean beetle could have seen that this was somebody's garden."

The giant hung his head.

The wee small woman gathered rosemary and basil and oregano and thyme to mix in the soup. She looked at what was left of her garden. A tear trickled down her face and splashed on the parsley.

"I'll have to plant another garden right away," she sniffed.

The giant looked up. "Maybe I could help," he offered.

"You?" snapped the wee small woman. "What could *you* do? Can you plant seeds?"

The giant broke up a tree for firewood. "No," he admitted, lighting the fire.

"Can you see to pull up weeds when they sprout between the plants?" demanded the wee small woman, sharply.

The giant shook his head.

"Can you pick potato bugs off the vines?" asked the wee small woman.

"No," the giant admitted. "But if cows get into the garden, I can carry them back to their field. And there's not a crow around would bother a garden with a giant in it." He frowned fiercely and flapped his arms.

"Well, you couldn't stay in *my* house,"
declared the woman with a wee small smile.
"There's scarcely room for me."

"That's true," agreed the giant cheerfully.
"But I could build a cottage down the lane
a piece."

The wee small woman stirred the soup. While it bubbled and simmered and sang, she considered. "I can plow and water and weed quite well by myself," she thought. "But it might be nice to have a friend."

She smiled a wide, wide smile as she filled a stewpot full of soup for the giant, and a bowl full of soup for herself.

Then she took off her apron and spread it on the ground for a tablecloth.

"All right," she said, picking up her spoon.

High over her head, Giant Rumbleton smiled, too.

"Soup with cabbage, soup with carrot—
A pot of soup and a friend to share it,"

sang the giant, sitting down and picking up his ladle.

"This is fine soup," he said, tasting it.

"Yes," the wee small woman agreed. "This is very fine soup indeed."

The Soup Song

Booming, like a giant

Chorus

Soup, soup, soup, a de- li- cious pot of soup,

Soup, soup, soup, I will eat it with a scoop—

Soup for sup- per to- night.

Verse 1

Soup with pars- nips, soup with peas,

Back to chorus

Soup with ru- ta- ba- gas, please.

Verse 2

Soup with onions, soup with parsley,
Soup with pepper sprinkled sparsely.

Chorus

Verse 3

Soup with cabbage, soup with carrot—
A pot of soup and a friend to share it.

Chorus

Lyrics by Phyllis Root

Music by Linda Sanders